DROOLING
AND
DANGEROUS
The Riot Brothers Return!

by MARY AMATO

illustrated by
ETHAN LONG

Holiday House / New York

For every reader who has written me a
letter saying, "I can't wait for your next book."
Thanks for the encouragement.
M. A.

For my brother, Alec,
whose drool is very dangerous
E. L.

Text copyright © 2006 by Mary Amato
Illustrations copyright © 2006 by Ethan Long
All Rights Reserved
Printed in the United States of America
www.holidayhouse.com
First Edition
1 3 5 7 9 10 8 6 4 2

Library of Congress Cataloging-in-Publication Data

Amato, Mary.
    Drooling and dangerous : the Riot Brothers return! / by Mary Amato ; illustrated by
Ethan Long.—1st ed.
        p. cm.
    Contents: The Riot Brothers become spies—The Riot Brothers star in a movie—
The Riot Brothers have a Dwitch Say.
    ISBN-13: 978-0-8234-1986-9 hardcover
    ISBN-10: 0-8234-1986-X hardcover
        1. Children's stories, American. 2. Brothers—Juvenile fiction. 3. Schools—
Juvenile fiction. 4. School principals—Juvenile fiction. [1. Brothers—Fiction.
2. Schools—Fiction. 3. School principals—Fiction. 4. Humorous stories.
5. Short stories.] I. Long, Ethan, ill. II. Title.

PZ7.A49165Dro 2006
[Fic]—dc22

2005052538

CONTENTS

Book One
THE RIOT BROTHERS BECOME SPIES

1

Book Two
THE RIOT BROTHERS STAR IN A MOVIE

63

NOV · 2006

Book Three
THE RIOT BROTHERS HAVE A DWITCH SAY

BONUS!

ONE

Thoink!

I, Wilbur Riot, happened to be squeezing a giant cockroach between my fingers when I made an important new discovery.

What is the new discovery, you ask?

Good question. I'll tell you in a minute. But first, I have some questions for you: Are you bored? Do you like exciting and dangerous adventures?

Well, you've opened the right book. We're the Riot Brothers, and we can't wait to tell you about our exciting—

Wait! I feel a Riot Brother saying coming on. Sayings come to me naturally because, for a fifth-grader, I am wise beyond my years. Actually, I feel several sayings coming on.

1. Riots are the best medicine.
2. A riot a day keeps boredom away.
3. Don't have a cow—have a riot!
   (Unless you need the milk.)

I can't decide which is best. Please vote for the one you like by writing it down on a trillion-dollar bill and mailing it to me, Wilbur Riot. (Just kidding. There's no such thing as a trillion-dollar bill—ha-ha.)

Anyway, where was I?

Oh yes! I was in my bedroom, making the cockroach's legs squirm by gently squeezing his shell. "I have made an important new discovery," I announced to my brother.

Orville grabbed the cockroach out of my hand. "You discovered a big bug in your bed?" He tossed it into the air, and it landed on my head . . . *thoink!*

"No!" I snatched the cockroach out of my hair. "I discovered the secret of a great game. The secret has to do with secrets." I stuffed the bug down Orville's pajama shirt.

Orville wriggled until the cockroach hit the floor . . . *thoink*! He grabbed it and dropped it down my pajama pants. For a third-grader, Orville is quick at catching bugs. "What's the secret, Wilbur?" he asked.

The cockroach tumbled down my bare leg and fell out of my pants . . . *thoink*! Before Orville could grab the cockroach again, I smooshed it with my foot. *Shmoink!*

If the poor thing weren't made of plastic, it would be dead by now.

"The secret of a great game," I explained, "is to keep the game a secret."

"But if it's a secret, how will I know how to play it?" Orville asked.

"We keep it a secret from grown-ups—not from each other. Let's make it a rule. Riot Brother Rule Number Eleven: Do not tell grown-ups how to play secret games."

"Okie dokie. What'll we play, Wilbur?"

"Let's invent a new dinner-table game!" I picked up the cockroach. "During dinner, we have to try to flip a bug across the table without Mom seeing it. The goal is to make it land in the other person's food. If my bug lands in your food, I get ten points."

Orville's eyes lit up. "And if my bug lands in your food, I get ten thousand points."

"Ha-ha. Okay. We both get ten thousand points."

Orville grabbed the cockroach and aimed at my trash can . . . *thoink*!

"Wait," I said. "This is going to be too easy. We have to use smaller bugs." I rummaged around until I found our box of plastic bugs.

6

"Let's use these. And we can't just throw them. We have to use a spoon to catapult the little buggies across the table."

"There's only one problem, Wilbur."

"What's that?"

"A catapult is for cats, not for bugs!" Orville laughed.

"Not too shabby of a joke, Orville."

"Thank you, Wilbur. Not too shabby of a game. What'll we call it?"

"Bye-Bye Buggie?" I suggested.

"That's it!" Orville threw the bugs in the air and started dancing around the room singing, "Bye-Bye Buggies. Don't get squashed on the ruggie." Then he stopped and frowned.

"There's only one more problem, Wilbur," he said sadly.

"What's that?"

"We have to wait until dinner to play it, and we haven't even eaten breakfast yet."

"There's a simple solution, little bro."

He grinned. "Invent a time machine so that we can zoom forward?"

"That's not a bad idea. But I was thinking we could play it at breakfast."

Orville patted me on the back. "I like the way you think."

I bounced a beetle off his head. "I like the way you thoink!"

He bounced a beetle off my head. "I like the way *you* thoink!"

I grabbed a spider and threw it. Orville ducked, and at that very moment our mom walked in. The spider got her right between the eyes . . . *thoink*!

She screamed, "What was that?" She saw

the spider on the ground and screamed again. For a plastic bug, it looked very real.

Perhaps I should take a moment here to say thank you to the Fake Bug Makers of the World for their talent and hard work. Great job, Bug Makers. Keep up the good work.

Back to the story. Mom squashed the spider. That's when she realized that it was plastic. She sighed and stared at us with her annoyed face.

I looked at Orville. "I'm afraid something is *bugging* our dear mother," I said.

Orville cracked up.

TWO
Bug Makers Rock!

Here's another one of my Riot Brother sayings: There's nothing like going to breakfast with bugs hidden in your pocket to get the day off to a great start.

I got a bowl of cereal. Orville got grapefruit and a piece of peanut butter toast. We brought our breakfast to the table, and Mom poured us each a glass of orange juice. She sat down with her tea and newspaper.

One of the reasons for my great success in life is that I do not waste time sitting around, wondering what to do. When I see an opportunity, I go for it. So when Mom opened her newspaper, I reached in my pocket and—

Sploink! A spider landed in my orange juice.

My brother had beaten me to it!

Orville's face was doing a victory dance. He was mouthing "ten thousand points" with a big grin. Mom lowered her newspaper to look at him, and he took a bite of his toast as if nothing had happened.

Mom returned to her newspaper.

My turn to get the O-bro!

Quietly, I spooned Orville's spider out of my juice and shot it.

Where did it land, you wonder? In Orville's juice? On his toast? On his grapefruit? Well, sometimes I am too strong for my own good. That spider zoomed clear across the table and over Orville's head.

Zoink! It hit the picture of Great Grandpa Riot on the wall.

Mom looked up. "What was that?"

"What?"

"That sound."

"I didn't hear anything, did you, Orville?"

"I didn't hear a thing, Wilbur."

Mom picked up her newspaper.

Sploink! A centipede splashed into my cereal bowl.

Orville's arms shot up like he had just scored a touchdown.

Mom caught him in the act. "What are you doing?"

Orville stretched his arms higher. "I'm doing my exercises. Stretch! Stretch! Stretch! Stretch!"

"Why are you doing exercises at the breakfast table?"

"It's National Exercise Day. You should stretch, Mom. You're really out of shape."

"I am not!" Mom stretched her arms in the air. "I'm in great shape."

"I bet you can't stand up and touch your toes," I said.

Mom stood up and bent over to touch her toes.

I was ready. I catapulted a spider over the napkin holder. It landed on Orville's toast!

"Excellent, Mom!" I said. "That toe-touch was worth ten thousand points!"

"Thank you, Wilbur," Mom said.

"I'll bet you can't twist around and look over your shoulder," Orville said.

She did it.

"That's good, Mom," I said. "Now stay there and count to ten."

While Mom was counting, Orville and I both stuck bugs on our spoons and fired. His bug landed in my lap. My bug landed on his toast.

"We're tied!" I whispered.

"What did you say?" Mom asked.

"We're tired," I said with a yawn. "Just watching you exercise makes us want to go back to sleep."

"Ha!" she said proudly. "I told you I was in good shape."

"Can you twist the other way and hold it for ten more seconds?" I asked.

"Sure!" When Mom twisted around, we loaded our spoons and fired again. In midair, our bugs crashed into each other. One bug landed on Orville's grapefruit, and the other *sploinked* into my cereal.

"We're still tied!" Orville whispered.

"I'm not tired," Mom said. Before she finished counting, I snuck in another shot—an ugly beetle. It landed in Mom's tea!

I was about to get it out when Mom sat back down. "I should stretch like that every morning. It feels great."

The beetle was bobbing in her teacup, just waiting to be seen. I needed Orville's help to get the beetle out without Mom seeing it. I gave him the secret signal to create a distraction. (Don't tell anybody, but the secret signal is to secretly point to the nearest window.)

Riot Brother Rule #12:
If one person is about to get in trouble,

the other person must create a distraction
outside the nearest window.

Orville jumped up and ran to the window. "Mom, look at that!"

When Mom turned around to look, I spooned the beetle out of her teacup.

"I don't see anything," she said.

"There was a squirrel out there doing jumping jacks!" Orville exclaimed. "Did you see it, Wilbur?"

"I certainly did. It was extraordinary, Orville!"

Mom laughed. "Either the squirrel knows that it's National Exercise Day, or you boys are seeing things. Now that I'm done exercising, I'm going to finish reading the paper." She picked up her newspaper.

I got my catapult ready. As I was about to fire, Orville reached over and knocked my elbow. The beetle flew sideways. It flew over

Mom's newspaper and landed on her head.

She screamed and jumped up. "What was that?"

There was only one thing for Orville and me to do: We laughed.

She shook her head. When the beetle fell out and landed on the table, she realized that it was another fake. She put her hands on her hips. "I should have known something fishy was going on," she said.

"You mean something buggie!" Orville laughed even louder.

She rolled her eyes. "I think one of you has something to say to me."

I was going to apologize for catapulting an insect into her hair so early in the morning. But Orville spoke up. For a third-grader, he often has something interesting to say.

"Mom," he said, "if you're finding bugs in your hair, I think you should shampoo more often."

THREE
Who Wants to Be a Chicken?

Mom didn't have time to get mad because it was time to leave for school.

We bundled up and headed out the door. We live close to our school. Sometimes we walk. Sometimes we drive. Today I guess we were walking.

Mom marched ahead of us. She was either getting her exercise or making sure that she was out of thoinking range.

"Orville," I said, "we have a problem."

"I know what the problem is," Orville said, his feet crunching on the snow. "It's freezing out here."

"That's a problem, but not the one I was thinking of."

"Then the problem must be that we don't have a private stretch limousine to take us to school."

"That's a problem, too. But not the one I was thinking of, either."

"Then the problem must be that we like to eat chicken fingers."

"That's not even a problem, Orville."

"It is if you're a chicken."

He had me there.

"I'll tell you the problem," I said. "The

problem is that it's time for school, and we haven't chosen our mission for the day."

"Do we have to choose a mission every day?"

"Is your brain filled with toast crumbs? Yes. It's Riot Brother Rule Number One: Make something exciting happen every day."

"Why don't we get kidnapped, Wilbur? That would be exciting. And then we wouldn't have to go to school."

"Perhaps you don't have a crummy brain after all. That's a fine idea. Except I don't know any kidnappers we can get to kidnap us."

Orville pulled his cap down. "How about if we become spies instead?"

I grinned. "That's it! We need code names. I'll call you Agent O. You call me Agent W."

Agent O nodded in a spylike way.

"We also need a password. Whenever I see you, you have to tell me the password so that I know that you are really you and not some enemy spy disguised as Agent O."

"Cool. What's the password?"

I thought a moment. It had to be something only Orville and I knew. "Bye-Bye Buggie," I whispered.

"I'll never forget it!"

Since our mom is the school principal, we have to go to school early every day. Usually we hate it. Today we liked it because it gave us plenty of time to spy.

"Where should we start?" Agent O whispered.

"Let's infiltrate the mail room! Teachers always check their boxes first."

"Excellent idea, Agent W. But what does *infiltrate* mean?"

"I don't know, but I'm sure we're good at it."

We hid behind two file cabinets in the mail room. There was a space between the file cabinets where we could see out.

We didn't have to wait long for action.

The kindergarten teacher came in, got her mail, and left.

The P.E. teacher came next, got her mail, and left.

"This isn't very exciting," Orville whispered.

"Shhh!"

Mr. Martin, the music teacher, came in. He didn't even look in his box. He looked nervously at his watch.

Agent O and I glanced at each other. Mr. Martin was up to something.

Mr. Peabody, my teacher, came in.

"I've been looking for you!" Mr. Martin whispered.

"Relax, Jack."

"I can't relax, Peter. I've never been so nervous in my life."

This was getting exciting. What was Mr. Jack Martin so nervous about? And why were they whispering? We held our breaths and listened.

"Everything's going to be fine," Mr. Peabody said.

"Do you have the diamond?" Mr. Martin asked.

Agent O gasped, and I put my hand over his mouth.

"It's perfect," Mr. Peabody said.

"Let me see it!"

"It's in my classroom."

"Classroom!"

"Stop worrying. It's safe. I'll hand it over to you at lunch, okay? Now stop worrying."

"I can't help it. I've never done anything like this before."

"Nothing's going to go wrong. I'll meet you in the teachers' lounge at 12:15."

"And you'll bring the diamond?"

"Of course!" Mr. Peabody patted Mr. Martin on the back. "Try to act like it's an ordinary day."

"Shhh! Somebody's coming, Peter. Let's go."

They left.

Agent O and I crept out from behind the file cabinets.

"What do you think is going on, Agent W?" Orville whispered.

"I think Mr. Peter Peabody and Mr. Jack Martin are international diamond smugglers."

"Bingo bongo. That's what I think, too. Should we go tell Mom?"

"No! Spies never tell their moms anything. We have to infiltrate the teachers' lounge and spy on them to get proof."

"We'll catch them in the act by using our Riot Brother Spy Camera and Voice Recorder."

"Yes! There's only one problem."

"I know. We don't have any spy gear. But there is a tape recorder in Mrs. Pensky's room."

"Great! See if you can borrow it without being seen."

The bell rang. We had to go to class.

"Meet me in the boys' bathroom at 12:05," I said. "Until then, we can't blow our cover."

"What's our cover?"

"We have to pretend we are just regular kids."

"Okie dokie, Wilbur."

"Spies don't talk like that, Orville."

"What should I say?"

"Say Roger."

"Okie dokie, Roger."

"No! Say my name."

"Okie dokie, Roger Wilbur!" Orville cracked up.

FOUR
Testing, Testing . . . Is This Thing On?

If you were a spy, and your teacher was an international diamond smuggler who was about to make a deal, wouldn't you have a hard time paying attention in class? I did. I wanted to freeze Mr. Peter Peabody with my Stop-Action Freezer Beamer and search his room for the diamond, but I didn't have a Stop-Action Freezer Beamer. Luckily, I did have a spy's most important tool: eyeballs.

With my sly spy eyes, I watched Peabody's every move. But of course, I looked without looking as if I was looking.

If Peabody knew that I was spying on him, he would probably send a counterspy to spy on me to find out what I know. And when that counterspy found out that I know all about the diamond, he'd tie me up and stuff me in the janitor's closet, which would not be good because the janitor's closet smells like wet mops, and I do not like the smell of wet mops.

Finally 12:05 rolled around. I asked Mr. Peabody if I could go to the bathroom.

"I'm dismissing you for lunch at 12:10. Can't you wait?" he asked.

I hopped up and down. "No."

"Fine. Go straight to the lunchroom from the bathroom."

My plan was working out exactly as planned.

I ran to the boys' bathroom.

Agent O was already there. Or at least it was somebody who looked like Agent O. It could have been one of Peabody's spies, wearing an Orville mask to trick me! In fact, this guy looked a little too fat to be Agent O. I took a step backward, ready to run out the door, if necessary. "What's the password?" I whispered.

"Hiya, Roger," he said loudly.

"That's not the password! And speak softly. This place might be bugged. Now, what's the password?"

"I don't know, Roger," he said.

"Stop calling me Roger. My name is Agent W and the password is Bye-Bye Buggie!" I clamped my hand over my mouth. "Oh man, I just gave it away."

"I'm glad you did because I could not remember it."

I looked at him more closely. "If you really are Agent O, why are you so fat?"

He pulled a tape recorder out from under

his sweatshirt and grinned. I guess he was the real Agent O.

"Want to know how I got it?" he asked.

The bell for lunch rang. "Tell me later. It's time to spy!"

We snuck down the hall and slipped into the teachers' lounge. We had no time to lose. Quickly we pulled the couch a few inches away from the wall and crouched down behind it. Good thing we're skinny.

I whispered, "Test the recorder to make sure it works, Agent O."

Orville cleared his throat and sang softly. "Old MacDonald had a farm. E–I–E–I–O!" He laughed and shut off the recorder.

The door creaked open, and we froze.

Footsteps grew louder and then stopped. My heart was beating fast. I looked at Orville.

His face was smooshed against the back of the couch. He was holding his breath.

Someone sat on the couch with a loud sigh. There was a moment of silence. The door creaked open.

"Peter!" Mr. Jack Martin jumped up from the couch. "Do you have it?"

We heard the sound of Mr. Peter Peabody's evil laugh. "Feast your eyes on this."

He must have handed over the diamond because Mr. Martin gasped. "Wow! It looks better than I imagined it. What a steal! I'm so glad you talked me into this."

"They're coming! If you don't want any-body to see it, you better put it away quick."

Orville and I looked at each other. We had it all on tape. When the Riot Brothers set out to do something, we do it!

Perhaps right now you are wondering what I was wondering. Do spies get rewards or bonus paychecks or free jumbo jets for uncovering international diamond smugglers? That's what I was wondering.

Unfortunately, I didn't have too much time to wonder because the door opened, and a herd of hippos came in. They weren't really hippos. They were teachers. But they sounded

like hippos. They were laughing and getting stuff out of the vending machines. We would have to wait until lunch was over before we could sneak out and take our proof to the FBI.

Now I bet you are wondering what teachers talk about in the teachers' lounge. I'll tell you what they talk about: They talk about *us*.

"Orville Riot was acting stranger than

usual," Mrs. Pensky said. "He wanted to borrow my tape recorder for a science experiment."

"That sounds educational," the science teacher said. "What was the experiment?"

"He said he was going to the boys' bathroom to record the sound of flushing."

Everybody laughed.

"He wants to see if the sound of flushing makes his goldfish scared."

Everybody laughed louder.

"He's very creative," Ms. Geary, the art teacher, said.

Orville shrugged and grinned.

"Wilbur was acting stranger than usual, too," Mr. Peabody said. "He was very fidgety. And every time I looked at him, he looked away. I think he did something bad and is feeling guilty."

How dare Mr. Peabody accuse me of being guilty of something bad! I jumped up from behind the couch. "I didn't do anything bad. But there are two people in this room who are guilty of something terrible. Right, Agent O?"

Orville jumped up. "Right, Agent W."

The teachers stared at us.

The door opened. Mom walked in, took one look at us, and groaned. "Now what's going on?"

"Although we look like ordinary kids, we are really spies," I explained. "And we have uncovered a diamond-smuggling plot. We were going to wait and present our proof to

the FBI. But we will let you hear the proof right now. Orville, rewind the tape."

Orville rewound the tape and pushed play. Everybody listened.

"Old MacDonald had a farm. E–I–E–I–O!" Orville's voice floated out of the tape recorder. After he was done singing, there was the horrible sound of nothing.

"Sorry, Wilbur." Orville winced. "I forgot to turn it back on."

Now what? Without proof, how would we prove anything? Wait a minute. We had proof! The proof was in Mr. Martin's pocket. I pointed to our music teacher. "Check that man's pocket. He has a diamond in it or my name isn't Agent Wilbur Riot."

Mr. Martin sighed. "Wilbur and Orville are right. I have a diamond in my pocket." He stood up and pulled a box out of his pocket.

The teachers were speechless. Even our mom was speechless.

"But I didn't smuggle it or steal it," he added. "I bought it from Peter Peabody whose brother Paul owns a jewelry shop called Paul's Jewel Box."

"I love that shop," Ms. Geary said.

Mr. Martin looked at her and then opened the box. A diamond ring sparkled. "I was going to do this on Valentine's Day," he said. "But I might as well do it right now." He walked over to Ms. Geary and kneeled. "Joan, I am deeply in love with you. Will you marry me?"

Ms. Joan Geary turned red and smiled. "Oh Jack!" She threw her arms around him and kissed him.

Everyone clapped and gathered around the happy couple.

Except us. We would have clapped and gathered, but we were too busy sneaking out. Besides, we don't like lovey-dovey stuff.

FIVE
How to Survive the Room of Doom

We snuck into the cafeteria, expecting Mom to grab us at any moment. There were only two minutes left for lunch. So we got our sack lunches from the big tubs in the cafeteria and sat down.

"Hey, where have you guys been?" Goliath Hyke asked.

"We can't say," I said.

Riot Brother Rule #2:
Do not tell anyone your true mission.

I took a bite out of my peanut-butter-and-jelly sandwich. Orville took a bite out of his.

Orville screamed and spit. "A bug!"

At that moment, my teeth hit something hard and crunchy in between the peanut butter and the jelly. "Ugh!" I screamed and spit. Six hairy legs were sticking out of my sandwich.

Goliath poked at the bug that Orville had spit out. "It's fake."

Everybody at the table laughed.

Just then, a voice came over the intercom. The voice of the principal. "Hello, boys and girls. It's time for third-, fourth-, and fifth-graders to have recess. Don't forget to clean your tables so that we don't attract any bugs."

The kids at our table laughed again.

"Mom put bugs in our lunch to get back at us for this morning!" Orville said.

I nodded. "She has learned from us too well."

"Man," Goliath said. "I didn't think the principal was that cool."

The intercom clicked on again. "Oh. And one last thing," she said. "Wilbur and Orville Riot, please come to my office."

"What did you do?" Jonathan Kemp whispered. "Are you in trouble?"

I'm afraid we were doomed.

As we walked to the principal's office, I got a brilliant idea. "Let's come up with a list of punishments for Mom to choose from."

Orville looked at me. "Are you crazy? Why would we want to come up with a list of punishments?"

I raised one eyebrow. "The punishments we think of will be better than hers."

Orville nodded. "Not too shabby, Wilbur. Let's do it."

We made a list of punishments.

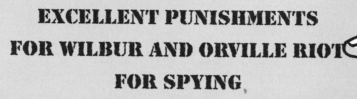

**EXCELLENT PUNISHMENTS
FOR WILBUR AND ORVILLE RIOT
FOR SPYING**

(Please choose one.)

1. The Riot Brothers must throw away all their spy gear.
2. The Riot Brothers must give up eating squash soup for the rest of their lives.
3. The Riot Brothers are not allowed to go to the Valentine Dance.

Don't tell our mom, but here's why we picked those punishments.

1. We don't have any spy gear!
2. We hate squash soup!
3. We'd rather eat squash soup than go to the Valentine Dance!

We were ready. We walked into her office and sat down.

She peered at us over her glasses. "Did you enjoy your lunch?"

We nodded.

"Good job with the bugs in our sandwiches, Mom," Orville said.

She smiled sweetly. "Thank you. But that's

not why you're here. Seriously, I want you to know that what you did today was really terrible. Mr. Martin could be very upset with you for ruining his surprise the way you did."

"We know. That's why we made a list of punishments for you to choose from." I handed her the list.

She read them over. "I think I'll choose number four."

"There is no number four," I said.

"Oh yes there is." She picked up a pencil and wrote, "The Riot Brothers will write letters of apology to Mr. Martin and Mr. Peabody. And there will be no more spying in school."

She handed it back to us.

"Got it?" she asked.

"Okie dokie, Roger Mom," Orville said.

SIX

What's in Your Garbage Can?

We wrote our letters of apology and delivered them after school. Then we went home, did our homework, ate dinner, and washed the dishes.

"Life is boring when you're not spying on someone," I said as I put the last plate in the dishwasher.

Orville wiped the salad bowl. "I miss the old excitement," he sighed.

"There's something that's really bugging

me, Orville," I said as I dried my hands on a dish towel. "And it's not the spider you just put down my back." I wriggled until the spider fell out. "I don't think we succeeded in our mission to become spies, because Mr. Peabody and Mr. Martin weren't guilty."

Orville picked up the spider and put it in the refrigerator. "I think we succeeded, because it was fun even if we did get in trouble."

"But I don't feel *complete,* Orville."

Orville thought for a moment. Then he leaned in and whispered, "Mom said we couldn't spy in school. She didn't say we couldn't spy here at home."

I nodded. "How right you are, Agent O. Let's get cracking."

First we spied on Mom. She was snoring on the couch. She doesn't snore like a regular mom; she snores like a horse with a fly up her nose. Kind of funny, but not too exciting.

Next we staked out the street from our bedroom windows. I looked out the front window. I like the way our street looks at night. It was about seven o'clock. Already dark. Circles of light from the streetlights made the snow glisten.

"I spy . . . Jonathan Kemp, walking home from his piano lesson," I said. He takes piano from a woman at the end of the block. Not too exciting.

Orville looked out the other window. "I spy . . . something's happening!" he exclaimed. "It's a . . . it's a . . . it's a . . ." He sighed. "I thought it was a squirrel doing jumping jacks, but it was just a tree branch falling."

Just then Mrs. Overhoser came out of her house. The Overhosers are mean, crabby people who live next door. For the past month, Mr. Overhoser has been mad because his garbage can keeps getting knocked over, and he blames us even though we are

not guilty. Why do grown-ups always blame kids for things we don't do? We don't go around saying that grown-ups are guilty when—oops. Never mind.

"Mrs. Overhoser is talking to Jonathan!" I said. We ran to our window that faces their house. "He's going inside! Why would Jonathan go inside?"

Orville's eyes got big. "Maybe Mrs. Over-hoser offered him candy."

"Why would she offer him candy?"

His eyes got bigger. "Because they're kid-napping him!"

We both stared out the window. Nothing happened for a few minutes. Then Mr. Over-hoser came out the back door. He is a big guy with no neck and bushy eyebrows and an even bushier mustache. He was struggling

with something heavy. It was hard to see in the dark. It looked like . . . a bag.

Orville and I gasped.

"Are you thinking what I'm thinking, Wilbur?"

"I'm thinking that they tied up Jonathan and stuffed him into that bag!"

Mr. Overhoser put the bag into his garbage can and wheeled it down to the curb.

"What'll we do?"

"Let's go save Jonathan before it's too late!"

Orville stuck a flashlight into his pocket. I grabbed Mom's digital camera.

"We'll take pictures so that Mr. Overhoser can't deny it!"

We raced downstairs, slipped on our coats, and tiptoed out the front door. Mr. Overhoser had already gone back inside.

The night air was freezing. Orville shivered. "Poor Jonathan. We have to get him out before he turns into an ice cube." We crept down our driveway.

"Shhh!" I stopped. "Did you hear something?"

We crouched behind our bushes. Orville

looked at the Overhoser's house. "All clear," he said.

"Come on, it was probably a squirrel."

After we crept close to the can, I whispered, "Jonathan, it's us. We know you're in there. Don't yell or he'll hear us."

We were about to lift off the lid when a voice boomed behind us.

"I GOT YOU!"

Orville and I screamed and knocked into each other. Two huge hands grabbed the backs of our coats.

"I knew it was you two messing with my can!"

It was Mr. Overhoser.

At that very moment, Mrs. Kemp opened her door across the street. "What's going on over there? Jonathan, is that you?"

"It's the Riot Brothers," Mr. Overhoser growled. "I caught them knocking over my garbage can."

"We weren't knocking anything over!" I yelled and tore myself away from the kidnapper's grip.

"Is Jonathan over there?" Mrs. Kemp asked. "He should be home from his piano lesson."

I looked at poor Mrs. Kemp, shivering on her front steps. We had to uncover Mr. Overhoser's horrible secret. "Your son is right here, Mrs. Kemp." I was about to step forward and take the lid off the garbage can when the door to the Overhoser house creaked open. We all turned to look. Out walked . . . Jonathan! He was humming a little tune and carrying a waffle maker.

"Hey guys," he said.

He wasn't tied up. He wasn't stuffed in the garbage can. He wasn't even in a bad mood.

"Hi, Mom," he called. "Mrs. Overhoser wanted to return this."

"Thanks, Betty!" Mrs. Kemp called out.

"Wait a minute!" Mr. Overhoser growled at us. "If you two didn't come over to mess with my garbage can, what are you doing here?"

"We came to get Jonathan," I said quickly. "To see if he can come over and play."

"How'd you know I was here?" Jonathan asked us. "What are you guys . . . spies?"

Orville grinned, and I elbowed him before he gave away our secret mission.

"Sorry, boys," Mrs. Kemp called. "Jonathan has to come home now."

"Okie dokie," Orville said.

Mr. Overhoser scowled and whispered, "I'll be watching you."

Jonathan and the grown-ups went back inside. The street was quiet again. As we walked back home, the day's events swirled around in my mind like snowflakes swirling around in the silent air. I sighed. "Orville, I'm depressed."

"How come, Wilbur?"

"Because we didn't succeed in our mission this time, either. Mr. Overhoser turned out to be not guilty, too. Just like Mr. Peabody and Mr. Martin."

"That's not our fault. We were awesome." Orville did a little slide on the icy sidewalk heading up to our front door. Then he turned around and grinned at me, as happy as a penguin. Sometimes I wish I were young again. The young are so easily amused.

I sighed. "Yes, Orville. We were sneaky. We were quick. We were brave. But we didn't succeed. I won't be able to sleep until we use our spy skills to catch somebody who is really, truly guilty of something."

At that moment, we both heard a rustling in the bushes by Mr. Overhoser's driveway.

"What was that?" Orville whispered.

We crouched behind our bushes. "Look, something is creeping out of the shadows," Orville whispered. "It's heading toward the Overhosers' driveway."

Yellow eyes flashed in the distance.

I set the camera on zoom and put the flash on. "When I give you the signal, shine the flashlight on it, Orville. And I'll take a picture."

We crept a little closer, not daring to breathe. The creature crept to Mr. Overhoser's garbage can and reached up. It was amazing how far it could stretch. It grabbed the rim of the garbage can and began to pull it over. I nodded to Orville. He turned on the flashlight, and I snapped!

The garbage-can bandit was a raccoon with a dark mask, a huge pot belly, and very dainty paws. As the flash went off, and the can tumbled to the ground, the raccoon looked at us, startled.

It scampered away as Mr. Overhoser's front door opened.

"Again? I can't believe it!" he yelled. "Come out, boys. I know it's you."

We stepped out from behind the bush.

"We have found the masked culprit, Mr. Overhoser. It's not us. It's a raccoon," I announced and held up the camera. "And we have the proof!"

Using the little display screen on the back of the camera, we showed Mr. Overhoser the picture of the raccoon. Mrs. Overhoser came out and looked at it, too. Then she made him apologize for blaming us.

Victoriously, we marched home. We did it! We did it! Two sly spies returning from one successful mission.

When we opened the front door, Mom woke up from her nap and yawned. "What were you boys doing outside?"

I looked at Orville. Orville looked at me.

"Just out watching a raccoon doing jumping jacks," Orville said.

Mom laughed.

I laughed, too. Now that we had succeeded, I was the opposite of depressed. I was inflated. I danced around the room. Orville joined in, and we crashed into each other. "What an exciting day!" I said.

"Almost as good as being kidnapped and missing school," Orville said. "So what'll we do now, Wilbur?"

I reached into my pocket and pulled out a trusty old cockroach. "I think we should thoink some bugs at each other," I said.

"I think it's thoughtful of you to think of thoinking," Orville replied.

"Thank you," I said. "I'm thrilled that you think it's thoughtful."

And so we thoinked until we were thoroughly through thoinking.

The End

BOOK TWO

THE RIOT BROTHERS STAR IN A MOVIE!

ONE

Who Invented Sleep, Anyway?

Don't you hate sleep? Sleeping at night is bad enough. But sleeping in the morning is just plain ridiculous. I want to wake up as early as possible so I don't miss anything, don't you? What if you were sleeping, and a giant meteor from outer space struck the earth? You'd miss it!

I, for one, am not willing to let even a pebble from outer space pass me by while I'm sleeping. That's why my brother Orville was born. To wake me up.

Riot Brother Rule #13:
Whoever wakes up first
has to wake the other.

This is especially important on Saturdays. Sleeping on Saturdays isn't ridiculous. It's ridiculous + ridiculous + ridiculous. (That's threediculous!)

Today, Orville woke me by standing next to my bed and poking me. "What is our mission for today, Wilbur?" he asked.

When I opened my eyes, I was looking right into Orville's eyes. Did you know that when you look at someone's eyes closely, you can see your own little face inside the other person's pupil? Try this right now unless it's dark. If it's dark, wait until morning and then try it.

Anyway, there I was, staring at my teeny

tiny face in Orville's eyes, when a smell drifted into my nose.

Orville's breath.

"For a third-grader, you have big, bad breath," I said.

Orville snarled up his face like a wolf. "All the better to huff and puff you with, my dear!"

Before he could huff and puff that smell farther up my nostrils, I yelled and dove onto Orville's bed. Orville yelled and jumped on me.

After a few minutes of yelling and jumping, we heard our mom's voice from the bottom of the stairs. "If you're going to break your legs, come down and eat your breakfast first."

Every once in a while, our mom says something that actually makes sense.

Orville started racing down the stairs.

"Wait!" I cried. A saying was coming to me. Orville stopped and listened politely.

I cleared my throat. "A bad day is like bad breath," I said. "It just gets worse unless you do something about it."

"Good one, Wilbur!" He jumped to the bottom.

"Wait!" I cried again. "We need a mission for the day."

"Let's do something funny with costumes and props." Orville put an empty trash can over his head and posed with his arms out.

"What are you supposed to be?" I asked.

"I'm an alien from Planet Crud." His voice sounded deep inside the trash can. "I'm armed, so watch out!"

"You're not armed."

Orville waved his arms around. "See these? I'm armed!" Orville karate-chopped toward me.

I pushed him back and grabbed socks out of the laundry basket in the hall. "Well, I'm from Planet Fud, and I've got socks, so watch out!"

Orville lifted up the trash-can helmet and asked, "What are you going to do with socks?"

"Sock you!" I yelled and threw my socks at him. He lowered his trash-can helmet just in time, and the socks bounced off his helmet. He ran into the kitchen. Unfortunately, he couldn't see where he was going, so he ran straight into the wall. *Kabam!*

"Crud," he said. "Your walls here on Planet Earth are very hard."

"Cut!" Mom said and took the trash can off his head. "This is not a prop. This is a trash can. When you clean your room after breakfast, you can fill it with trash. Isn't that a great idea?"

I grabbed Orville and pulled him back into the hallway. "Mom just gave me a great idea for a mission!"

He looked at me in horror. "It doesn't have to do with cleaning our room, does it, Wilbur?"

"No," I whispered. "She gave me the idea when she said 'cut'!"

Orville grabbed his hair. "Don't tell me you want to get haircuts."

"No." I held up my hands like a movie director, framing a shot. "Our mission will be to star in a movie."

Orville nodded. "Not too shabby. I'll do it on one condition."

"What's that?"

"No lovey-dovey stuff. I only like funny movies."

"Of course! Let's shake on it."

We looked each other in the eye. We started to shake hands and karate-chopped instead. "Hiiiiiiya!"

"I said cut," Mom called out from the kitchen.

"We're not cutting; we're chopping!" Orville cried. "Hiiiiiiya!"

TWO
The Flight of the Whitey—Tighties

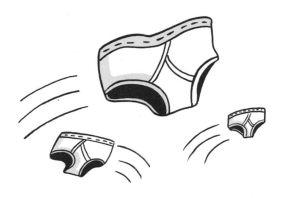

Since it was a Saturday, we had chocolate-chip pancakes for breakfast. We only get chocolate-chip pancakes on Saturdays, so we always eat one for each day of the week to make up for it. Then we feel sick from eating too much. If our mom would just make chocolate-chip pancakes every day, we wouldn't have this ridiculous problem.

We were in the dining room, eating pancakes faster than our mom could flip them. From the kitchen, she called out, "After breakfast, why don't you guys get busy cleaning your room?"

"We can't," Orville said with his mouth full. "We're going to star in a movie."

"Orville!" I whispered. "You just broke Riot Brother Rule Number Two!"

"Don't talk with your mouth full?" he asked with his mouth full.

"I like that rule," Mom said as she brought in another plate of pancakes.

I waited until she returned to the kitchen. Then I whispered, "No! That's not a Riot Brother Rule! Rule Number Two is: Do not tell anyone your true mission. I think we need a new rule. Riot Brother Rule Number Fourteen: You have to pay a fine for every rule you break."

"How much?"

"I think five thousand dollars sounds fair."

"Okay, Wilbur. But if you break a rule, you have to pay me five thousand dollars, right?"

"Sounds fair to me."

Orville sighed. "Since I'm going to be paying you five thousand dollars, would you mind getting me more milk?"

Thinking about all that money put me in a good mood, so I went to get Orville some more milk. When I returned, Orville jumped up and did a victory dance. "You owe me five thousand dollars, Wilbur! You just broke a rule when you walked in here. Riot Brother Rule Number Four: Run, do not walk, whenever possible." He laughed.

It's a sad day when your little brother starts to actually get smart. "Okay. Okay. No fines. But there should be a consequence."

Orville raised one eyebrow. "How about if we have to dance and squawk like a plucked chicken every time we break a rule?"

"Sounds fowl to me," I said, which made Orville crack up.

"Bawk! Bawk!" We started squawking and flapping and hopping around the dining room.

Mom walked in. "Where is a movie camera when you need one?" She sat down with her own pancakes and opened the news-paper. "Speaking of movies, look at this." She pointed to an advertisement and read, "'Come to the Grand-Opening Celebration of Hollywood Flicks video store at the Gate-way Shopping Mall and get a free raffle ticket. You could win a trip for two to Hollywood!' I'll take you boys after you clean your room. I need to do a little shopping anyway."

"We don't really want to become movie stars." I winked at Orville. "In fact, we're not going to have a mission today. But it might be fun to go to the shopping mall anyway."

"What do you mean we're not going to have a mission?" Orville got all red in the face. "It's a rule! We have to have a mission every day. You said so."

I turned my back to Mom and gave an extra jumbo wink to Orville. "I said we're not having a mission today. Let's go clean our room, Orville."

Orville's eyes bugged out. "Are you crazy? I don't want to clean."

I pulled him into the living room and whispered, "Didn't you see me give you the Opposite Wink? That means I'm saying the opposite of what I really mean."

"Oh." Orville grinned. "I get it!"

"What are you two whispering about?" Mom asked.

We ran back into the dining room. "Orville was just saying that he can't wait to clean, right, Orville?"

Orville jumped up and down. "Cleaning is fun!"

Now it was Mom's turn for buggie eyes.

We ran upstairs.

Orville opened his underwear drawer and started throwing his whitey-tighties into the air.

"What are you doing?"

"The opposite of cleaning!" He winked, and then he turned his laundry basket upside down. "This is a great idea, Wilbur. I love messing things up." He kicked a pile of dirty clothes. "Whee!"

"Stop! Orville, you still don't get it. I was winking about not having a mission. We do have a mission—to star in a movie. The first step is to win that trip to Hollywood."

He sat on his bed. "Can't our mission be to mess up our room?"

"No. Rule Number Five is: Don't change your mission in the middle of the day."

"Who made up these stinkin' rules, anyway?"

"We did."

"Oh yeah!" Orville grinned. "Let's stuff this junk under my bed and go win that trip to Hollywood."

THREE
Two Raffle Tickets, Hold the Syrup!

As soon as we got to the Gateway Shopping Mall, Mom went to one of those stinky lotion stores. Of course, it wasn't called the Stinky Lotion Store, it was called the Smelly Slime Shop. Ha-ha!

She let us go off on our own as long as we promised to meet her by the fountain in the central plaza in an hour.

We went to the video store right away. In front of the store was a table with a big RAFFLE sign, and balloons were all over the place. In the display window, a movie was showing on a giant screen: two funny guys, chasing each other down a busy street. "Take a look at that, Orville. Sometime soon, we're going to be on that silver screen. I feel lucky. Do you feel lucky?"

Orville poked himself all over. "I don't know, Wilbur. Do I *feel* lucky to you?"

"Good one, O-bro."

"Thank you, Wil-bro."

"Let's go to the raffle table."

"I don't want a waffle, Wilbur. I'm still full from all those pancakes."

"It's a raffle. Not a waffle. A raffle is like a lottery. You get a ticket with a number on it. And if they pick your ticket, you win. They're giving away *free* tickets. That's what we're here for."

"Oh yeah!" Orville said.

I stepped up to the table. Sitting behind it was a high-school girl who had obviously shopped at the Smelly Slime Shop because she smelled like slime. "Hi! Thanks for coming to our grand-opening celebration," she said. "Would you answer a few questions for us to get your raffle tickets?"

"We just want to get the tickets," Orville said. "Gimme three hundred please."

"Sorry." The girl shook her head. "One ticket per customer."

"Crud," Orville said.

"We'll take the questionnaire and get our two tickets," I said. "Fire away."

She picked up a clipboard. "What are your names?"

"Wilbur and Orville Riot," I said.

She raised her eyebrows. "You've got to be kidding."

Orville grinned. "It's really us."

She shrugged and wrote our names down. "And where are you from?"

"From Planet Earth," Orville said.

"Could you be more specific?" she asked.

"We're from here," I said.

"We are?" Orville grinned. "I didn't know we lived here. We have a very big movie screen in our house. Do you live here, too?" he asked the girl.

Like many people who live on Planet Earth, she didn't know what to make of Orville.

She wrote something down and asked the

next question. "How did you hear about the grand opening?"

"Our mom saw it in the newspaper," I said.

"The last question is this: In two words, how would you describe our new store?"

"In two words . . ." Orville said, ". . . delightful."

She handed us two tickets and two lollipops. "Thank you for coming to Hollywood Flicks. Next!"

We walked away and looked at our tickets.

"Two tickets isn't very many, Wilbur," Orville said. "We need more tickets to have a better chance."

I agreed. Then I realized something. "We're actors, Orville! We can disguise ourselves and get another ticket."

"Bingo bongo!"

FOUR

Lulubelle Lippi Likes Lollipop Lips

If you ever want to change your identity, try this little trick. One person sits on another person's shoulders. The person on top wears a long coat that covers up the person on the bottom so that you look like one tall person.

Orville and I found a long, poofy purple coat and a flowered hat in the Lost and Found bin next to the mall restrooms. Orville put on the hat and coat, and hopped up on my shoulders. The coat covered me so that I couldn't see a thing. "We'll only get one ticket,

but at least it will work," I said. "How do we look?"

Orville made his voice sound like a Southern woman's voice. "All I can see of you is your feet, darlin'. But I look purtier than a pig on a platter. Wait! I have a red lollipop in my pocket. I'll lick it and rub it on my lips so it looks like I've got lipstick on."

"Let's go! You weigh as much as ten pigs on a platter." I turned around and smacked straight into the bathroom door. *Bam!*

"Ouch!" Orville cried. "Watch where you're going, honey bun! Or you'll give Lulubelle a knock on the noggin."

"Who's Lulubelle?"

"I'm Lulubelle!" Orville said. "For a pair of feet, you sure don't have any brains."

Lulubelle opened the door, and I stumbled through.

"Go right, darlin'. Now go left. No! Go straight ahead." Lulubelle kept whispering and digging her heels into my sides.

"Ouch! Stop kicking me," I whispered back. "What do you think I am?"

"Why, you're my little ole horse. Giddyap, little horsey. We're almost there."

"For once, I wish I was the little brother and you were the big brother. Then I could be digging my heels into you!"

"Well, ain't it my lucky day? Now slow down and hush up, honey bun!"

I was distracted because I had to sneeze. I realized that the puffy coat probably had goose feathers in it. I'm allergic to goose feathers. "Lulubelle, I have to sneeze," I whispered.

"Shhh!"

Just then, I bumped into the raffle table, and Orville almost lost his balance.

"Whoa! Hello there, darlin'," Orville said in his high voice.

"Hello, ma'am," Raffle Girl replied. "Thanks for coming to our grand-opening celebration. Would you like to answer a few questions for us and get a raffle ticket? There's only twenty minutes left until we draw the winning ticket."

"Why certainly, sugar pie."

"What's your name?"

"My name is Lulubelle."

"And your last name?"

"Uh . . . Lippi. Lulubelle Lippi. Do you like my lipstick? It's called Lollipop Red. Ain't that cute?"

"Yes. It's very cute."

"Bet you can't say 'I like Lulubelle Lippi's Lollipop Lipstick' ten times real fast."

"I don't think I can. Where are you from, Ms. Lippi?"

"Why I'm from Mississippi."

"You're Lulubelle Lippi from Mississippi?"

"That's right, darlin'. Ain't that just the cutest name? Whenever I say it, my little old feet just want to dance around."

I danced around, and Orville sang Lulubelle's name over and over.

"Yes. It's very cute," Raffle Girl said. "How did you hear about the grand opening?"

"I heard about it from my cousin, Wilburina. She's real purty, too. She has feet that look just like mine!"

I stuck out one foot and wiggled it. My nose was tickling like crazy, but I held the sneeze in.

Raffle Girl continued. "In two words, how would you describe our new store?"

"Purty cute!" Lulubelle said.

I couldn't hold the sneeze in any longer. "Aaaaachooo!"

Through a little gap in the coat, I could see the Raffle Girl peering at Orville. "Did a sneeze just come out of your belly button?" she asked.

"Why yes! That's how we sneeze in Mississippi," Orville said and smooshed my nose.

I couldn't help it. Another sneeze came out.

Orville laughed. "I'm purty sneezy today, ain't I? Can I have my ticket now?"

As soon as I heard Orville say thank you, I turned and ran as fast as I could.

"Turn right!" Orville whispered. "Turn left. No . . . no . . . turn more . . . quick . . . no!"

I stumbled. My knees hit something hard, and I tripped.

Splash!

The coat was off my head. I stood up.

Lulubelle was in the fountain!

FIVE

Googoo Drool Drool

"You're purty wet," I said and pulled Orville out.

He grinned. "Got another ticket!"

We hurried to the restroom to dry Orville off and return the coat to the Lost and Found. On the way, we saw the mall's baby strollers, and I had another brilliant idea. The strollers in the mall are big and shaped like little red cars.

"Orville, do you think you can fit into one of those?"

Orville grinned. "Yeah! Let's borrow more costumes from the Lost and Found."

I borrowed a suit coat, tie, and hat. Orville borrowed a white baby blanket and climbed in the stroller. I tucked the blanket around him and began to push.

"This is fun," Orville said in a baby voice. "Push me faster, Daddy!"

I pushed. "You need to lose weight, little baby."

A few people looked at us. I think some of

them felt sorry for me because I had such a big baby.

"I want ice cream," Orville screamed as we passed by the ice-cream shop.

"No. Besides, you're too little to know how to talk!"

"Waaah!" Orville cried.

"Be quiet, you big ugly baby."

Orville banged his fists on the stroller. "Waaaah!"

"We're almost there. So be a good baby and go to sleepy. If you don't be quiet, I'm going to leave you in the Lost and Found."

I strolled up to Raffle Girl and straightened my tie.

"Hello, young lady," I said in a fathery voice. "I'd like two raffle tickets. One for me, and one for my baby. And I'm in a hurry because my baby has a very stinky diaper, as I'm sure you can tell." I pointed at Orville. "Bad baby!"

"Waaaah!"

"Stop crying, baby."

"Dada, Dada," Orville made little whispery sounds.

Raffle Girl said, "I think your baby is trying to tell you something."

I leaned closer.

"Bad dada!" Orville yelled and pinched my nose.

The girl laughed.

"Ha-ha." I smiled and pinched Orville's cheek. "You are a very funny baby, aren't you? Now don't do that again!"

Raffle Girl picked up her clipboard. "What's your name?"

"My name is . . . Frank Furter Fuddy-duddly."

"That's a long name."

I shrugged. "You can call me Mr. Frank F. Fuddyduddly for short."

"What's your baby's name?"

"Crud."

"You named your baby Crud?"

I nodded. "Crudly is his real name. Crudly Fuddyduddly. But we call him Crud for short."

"Doodoo baba!" Crud said. He grabbed the girl's clipboard and started banging it on the table. "Doodoo baba!"

"Be a nice baby, Crud!" I grabbed the clipboard and handed it to the girl.

"Crud is certainly a big strong baby," she said.

"Ba ba ba!" Crud drooled and banged his fists on the stroller.

"Where are you from, Mr. Fuddyduddly?"

"We live on . . . Muddypuddly Street."

Crud started waving his white blanket. "Mud, mud, pud, pud!" He laughed.

She wrote down my answer. "And how did you hear about the grand opening?"

"How did we hear about it? Well, we Fuddy-duddlys have very big ears."

Crud pulled his ears out and squealed.

"In two words, how would you describe our new store?"

"Jolly goodly, I'd say. Wouldn't you, Crudly?"

"Goo goo goo!" Crud grinned and drooled.

SIX
Say Cheese

I grabbed two tickets out of Raffle Girl's hands and said goodbye.

"We're going to announce the winners in a few minutes," Raffle Girl said.

"We'll be right back." I pushed Baby Crud back to the baby-stroller parking lot.

Orville hopped out. "That was fun! What should we be next? We could pretend we're exterminally ill!" Orville coughed and slumped to the floor. "Please give us some tickets, Raffle Girl! We just want to see Hollywood before we die!"

"They're going to pick the ticket. Come on; we've got to go."

We returned our costumes to the Lost and Found and ran back to the video store.

The owner was standing with a microphone on a little platform in front of the store. "Ladies and gentlemen," the owner called out to the passing crowd. "We're just about to draw the lucky winner of our Trip to Hollywood Raffle."

We crammed into the crowd and got out our tickets. We had five tickets. One of them had to be the winner.

The owner reached into a big tub of tickets and pulled one out. "The winning raffle ticket is: 55555443229754389914569998721."

"Is it ours?" Orville asked.

You know that feeling you get when you're about to win something? Well, the woman next to me must've had it because she started yelling and jumping up and down.

"I won!" she yelled.

Everybody clapped, and the owner gave her a big, glittery envelope that had tickets and stuff in it.

"I can't believe we didn't win," Orville said sadly.

"Come on; let's go."

We were just about to leave when the owner returned to the microphone. "And now we'd like to announce the surprise winners of our new Secret Hidden Camera Contest!

That's right! Our hidden camera has been rolling all day long, and we'd like to award the stars of the funniest clips with a case of Cheezie Pop microwave popcorn.

"Take a look at the screen." He pointed to the giant movie screen, hanging in the display window. "Roll it!"

There, on the screen, was Lulubelle stumbling up to the raffle table.

The crowd laughed.

"Hey, Wilbur, it's us!" Orville screamed.

The camera had caught everything, even our exit and Orville's big splash in the fountain. When it was done everybody clapped.

"That was us!" Orville yelled.

The owner saw us and waved at us to come up.

"Here they are, ladies and gentlemen!"

The crowd cheered when we hopped up on the platform.

"Roll the next clip!" the owner cried.

More people gathered around the display

window as they played our next scene, starring Mr. Fuddyduddly and his ugly baby, Crudly!

Everybody loved us! When it was over, the owner shook our hands. "What are your names?" He put the microphone in front of me.

"I'm Wilbur. And this is my brother, Orville. We are the Riot Brothers."

"The Riot Brothers!" He handed us a big box of Cheezie Pop popcorn. "You certainly are a riot. Give these stars another hand, ladies and gentlemen!"

Everyone clapped, and we bowed.

"Now that you are famous movie stars, what are you going to do next?" the owner asked.

"We're going to eat a lot of popcorn!" Orville said.

SEVEN
Who Wants an Autograph?

Even famous movie stars have mothers who get mad when they're late. So we had to run to meet Mom at the fountain.

"Where did you get that huge box of popcorn?" she asked.

"We won it!"

"How?"

"For being movie stars."

Mom gave us one of her I-don't-believe-it looks.

Just then a little boy with a broken arm came running up. "Hey, you guys are the stars of that funny movie. Will you autograph my cast?" He held out a pen.

Our mom's mouth dropped open.

Orville and I looked at each other and grinned. "Sure!" I told the boy. We signed our names on his cast. Then we told Mom the whole story of the Secret Hidden Camera Contest. We took her back to the video store, where they were still running clips of our famous scenes.

We stayed and signed autographs for a while. Then it was time to go home.

What a day!

To celebrate, we had pizza and popcorn for

dinner. Mom made a fire in the fireplace. We sat in front of it and watched the flames roar and hiss. If I had a pet dragon, I'd let it sleep in the fireplace and breathe fire all winter.

Anyway, we sat in front of the fire and tried to make sneezes come out of our belly buttons. And Mom told us the best stories, which are the ones about the funny stuff we did when we were little. Orville and I were wacky back then.

After the fire died down, Mom marched us up to bed.

"We're stars," I argued. "We can't go to sleep. We're going to shine all night long."

"Shine with your eyes closed," she said and turned out the lights.

I waited until she was gone, then I turned on my flashlight.

"Wow, you really are shining with your eyes closed, Wilbur," Orville whispered.

"It's my flashlight, Orville. Get yours and let's play What's My Dumb Problem, Chum?"

What's My Dumb Problem, Chum? is the name of an acting game that we invented on a long car ride. It's sort of like charades, except you can use sound effects. You pretend you have a big, stupid problem, and the other person has to guess what it is. If you play it in the dark, you have to shine flashlights on each other like spotlights.

"You guess first," I said. "I've got a good one." Orville shined his light on me. I bulged out my eyes, stuck out my tongue, and groaned.

"You're being squashed by an elephant named Lulubelle?" he asked.

"Nope."

"You're being kissed by a hippo with pink lipstick and bad breath?"

I laughed. "Nope."

"You're being forced to chew the dirty toenails of an alien life-form from the Planet Crud?"

"Gross! No! I'm being forced to eat Mom's squash soup."

"I heard that," Mom called out from the hallway.

"I told you Mom has big ears."

"I heard that, too," Mom said. "My ears are perfectly normal. And my squash soup is excellent."

"Her ears might be normal," Orville whispered to me, "but her taste buds are cruddy."

"I heard that, too. And with my big X-ray eyes, I can see through the wall that you guys need to turn off your flashlights and go to sleep."

I looked at Orville. Orville looked at me. How did she know we had our flashlights on?

The door to our room creaked open. Quickly, we turned off our flashlights.

"You really do have big eyes, Mom," Orville said.

"All the better to see you with, my dears!" she said and tickled Orville under his chin, which always gets him going. He laughed like a big, gurgly baby.

It's fun being all cozy in bed and listening to your brother laugh like a big, gurgly baby in the dark. I'm glad we were able to accomplish our mission of becoming movie stars without going to Hollywood. I like it here in Riot Land.

"Hey, Mom," I said. "Sorry we don't like your squash soup. I'm sure somebody does."

"It would probably be a big hit on Planet Crud," Orville added helpfully.

"Gee thanks, guys," Mom said.

"And thanks for taking us to the shopping mall today," I added.

"You're welcome." She pulled my blanket up. "That was quite an adventure."

"And thanks for starting the fire in the fireplace tonight," Orville said.

"Yeah. Thanks, Mom," I said. "Because if you didn't start it in the fireplace, our house would have burned down purty quick!"

Orville and Mom both cracked up.

"Wait!" Their chuckles gave me an idea for a saying. I sat up in bed and cleared my throat. "I have another saying," I announced. "You should always laugh before you go to bed. If you have to go to bed before you've had a good laugh, call us, and we'll come right over!"

Orville clapped. "Good one, Mr. Fuddy-duddly."

I bowed. "Why thank you, Lulubelle!"

The End

P.S. I asked my mom if I could print our phone number so you could call us, but she said nope. So I have to change my saying: You should always laugh before you go to bed. If you have to go to bed before you've had a good laugh, try to crack yourself up first.

BOOK THREE

THE RIOT BROTHERS HAVE A DWITCH SAY

ONE

I've Got a Headegg!

Have you ever had a great idea ready to burst out of your brain? Well, I have. And I'll tell you what it feels like: It feels like your head is an egg and there's a big bird in there that's trying to get out.

The other day, I woke up with an idea bursting out of my head, and here's what I did: I hopped out of bed and jumped on my brother's head. "Orville, wake up!!!"

Orville leaped out of bed so fast that his pajama pants fell off. In a panic, he ran around, flapping his arms like *he* was a big bird. "IS THE HOUSE ON FIRE? ARE WE

BEING KIDNAPPED? IS A TORNADO COMING?"

"Orville, stop flapping and put your pants on! Nothing bad is happening."

He looked disappointed.

"I woke you up because I know what our mission is going to be today."

"It better be a good one," he said.

"It is! We're going to have a Switch Day. All day, we switch stuff. Switch places. Switch clothes. Switch everything we can think of."

"That's a great idea." Orville's eyes lit up. "We could switch wallets!"

"That's a horrible idea. I have way more money than you."

Orville rubbed his hands together and raised one eyebrow. "What if we switched wallets with Mom?"

"Now that's a fabulous idea." I jumped on Orville's bed. "The *Biot Rrothers* are having a *Dwitch Say*!"

"What?"

"I'm switching letters, get it? The *Biot Rrothers* are having a *Dwitch Say*."

"I get it!" Orville jumped on my bed. "Hurray for *Dwitch Say*!"

"Let's do some switching right now."

"Yeah!"

I jumped off the bed. "Remember, we have to keep this a secret from Mom."

"Bingo bongo!" Orville said and saluted.

"You mean *bongo bingo!*" I said and saluted back. "Hopefully Mom is still asleep." For some reason, Mom often likes to sleep late on Saturdays, which can come in handy for us.

We tiptoed down the stairs and peeked into Mom's room. Her face was smooshed against her pillow, and her eyelids were closed. Her hair looked like it was hit by a hurricane. She looked like a disaster. She looked like a wreck. She looked like she needed immediate medical attention.

Orville gave the thumbs up.

"It's a good thing that grown-ups sleep with their eyes closed because it's much easier to have fun when they aren't watching," I whispered.

Orville nodded. "Now let's *set gwitching*."

TWO
Wake Up and Read Your Coffee

As quietly as pythons, we slithered through the house, switching this and that.

I know what you're thinking: You want to know exactly what we switched. Here's the list.

SECRET SWITCHES

1. We put socks in the tissue box and tissues in our sock drawers.
2. We put games in the pots-and-pans cabinet and pots and pans in the games cabinet.
3. We put cookies in the spaghetti box and spaghetti in the cookie jar.
4. We put toothbrushes in the forks drawer and forks in the toothbrush holder.

To make things even more exciting, we split up for some secret, secret switching.

MY SECRET, SECRET SWITCHES

1. I put rocks in Orville's candy box and candy in his rock collection box.
2. I put the snow shovel in the broom closet and the broom on the back porch.
3. I put Mom's underpants in Orville's drawer. And I had just finished putting Orville's underpants in Mom's drawer when she woke up.

Mom groaned and rubbed her eyes. "Why on earth are you wearing Orville's clothes?" (Did I mention that we switched clothes?)

Orville heard her and ran in.

Mom looked at him and added, "And why are *you* wearing Wilbur's clothes?"

Orville pulled me aside and whispered, "If we're switching everything around that means Mom is a kid and we're the bosses."

"You're switching things around, eh? I like that." Mom got out of bed. "That means you can make me breakfast."

I sighed. It's hard to keep secrets when you've got a brother with a big mouth and a mother with big ears.

Mom kept talking. "After breakfast, I get to watch cartoons while you two scrub the kitchen floor."

I turned to Orville and whispered. "See, this is just one reason why we need to keep our true missions a secret. Grown-ups have a way of adding a cleanup session to every mission. Anyway, you broke Rule Number Two again, so according to Rule Number Fourteen, you have to dance and squawk like a chicken."

Orville argued, "Since we're switching everything around, then we shouldn't keep the mission a secret."

"What can I say? Smart thinking, Orville."

Mom put on her slippers. "I'd like bacon and waffles with strawberries on top, please."

"Watch your attitude, little missy," Orville said.

I patted her on the head. "She needs our help, Orville. I'll make your breakfast, Lydia, if you promise to eat it all up."

Orville laughed and patted Mom on the head, too. "I'll make coffee for Wilbur and me!"

While Orville made coffee, I brought our mom a bowl of cereal and some juice in a sippy cup.

"Gee, thanks," she said.

"*Wou* are *yelcome,*" I replied.

After a few minutes, Orville came in with two steaming cups. "What do you think, Wilbur? Did the coffee turn out okay?"

I looked at it. I sniffed it. "Looks like mud. Smells like crud. Thanks, Orville!"

"*Po nroblem,*" he replied.

I handed him a section of the newspaper, and he sat down, pushed up his sleeves, and stared at his coffee.

"Don't tell me you're going to drink it," Mom said.

"It's *Dwitch Say.* I'm going to *read* my coffee. And Wilbur is going to *eat* his newspaper!"

I glanced at the paper. "Looks like the news today is very tasteless. Since it is *Dwitch Say,* I think we can have *bessert* for *dreakfast.*"

"*Bessert* for *dreakfast,*" Orville exclaimed. "*Bongo bingo!*"

"And since it's *Saturday*," I said. "We must have *sundaes*. Let's get the ice cream."

"Ice cream for *dreakfast*!" Mom laughed. "This *Dwitch Say* is *foing* to be *gun*."

I looked at my brother. "Did she say that *Dwitch Say* is *foing* to be *gun*?"

Orville nodded. "And she didn't even roll her eyes."

I stared Mom down. "Let me get this straight, little missy. Are you saying that you're going to go along with all this?"

Mom stood up and cleared her throat. "I feel a saying coming on," she announced, "because for a little missy, I'm good at making up sayings. Here it is: If you can't *jeat* them, *boin* them."

I looked at Orville. Orville looked at me.

"*Sot* too *nhabby*, Mom!" we both said at the same time.

Mom laughed. "Is it okay if I get dressed now?"

That reminded me of one of my secret,

secret switches. "Absolutely! Don't forget to put on clean underpants, Lydia!" I called out as she walked into her bedroom. I poked Orville and said, "Watch this."

Mom came out with Orville's underpants on her head. "I don't think these will fit."

Orville and I laughed.

"Exactly how many things around this house did you switch?" she asked.

"*Mot nany*," I said.

She put Orville's underpants on my head. "Today is going to be a *dacky way*."

THREE
That's So Funny, I Have to Cry

While Mom got dressed, Orville and I decided to go outside and play.

We put on our *cats* and *hoats* and went out the back door.

It was a cold, white winter wonderland out there. We stood in the snow for a while in complete silence and watched two crazy squirrels chase each other along the top of our fence. I should say that it wasn't a complete silence. Our noses were very noisy. We couldn't stop sniffing.

Did you ever notice how when you go out

in the cold, your nose starts to run? Why is that? Usually cold weather freezes things. Wouldn't you think that cold weather would make your snot freeze inside your nose?

"Wait!" I stopped and wiped my nose on my sleeve. "I have a saying."

Orville listened politely.

I cleared my throat and sniffed. "Snot and kids have a lot in common. When the weather is cold and snowy, they both like to come out and play!"

Orville started to cry.

"What's so sad about that?" I asked.

"It isn't sad. It's funny. But since it's *Dwitch Say*, I have to cry," Orville wailed.

The squirrels stopped and looked at

Orville, then they started chasing each other again.

"What is the point of their frantic antics?" I asked.

"I don't know what frantic antics are," Orville said, "but that reminds me of a great game."

"What's that, Orville?"

"*Gox* and *Foose!*" he replied. "I'll be the *Gox*." He started chasing me. *Gox* and *Foose* is a game of tag that you play on a path that you've made in the snow.

We played *Gox* and *Foose,* and our noses ran faster than we did. When we went inside, Orville yelled. "Mom, we need tissues!"

As we were taking off our wet *cats* and *hoats*, Mom walked into the kitchen with the tissue box and pulled out . . . one of my dirty socks. "What is this?" she asked.

"A *sirty dock*," Orville answered.

"Of course," she said. "Why did I even have to wonder?"

"We're hungry. Can we have lunch?" Orville asked. "How about frozen pizza?" he suggested with a big grin.

Mom took a pizza box out of the freezer, opened it, and pulled out . . . a Frisbee.

Orville laughed. "That was one of my secret, secret switches!" he said.

I patted him on the back. "Good one, Orville." Then I turned to Mom. "Why don't we have a big pot of spaghetti instead?" I suggested.

Mom opened the pots-and-pans cabinet and four games fell out.

We laughed again.

"Let me guess," Mom said. "The pots and pans are in the games cupboard?"

"Bongo bingo!" Orville ran to the cupboard to get a pot.

When he came back, Mom filled it with water and set it on the stove. When it was boiling I handed her the box of spaghetti. "Do you boys want a lot or a little?" she asked.

"A lot!" we both said.

She opened the box and . . . chocolate chip cookies tumbled out. Half of them fell into the water; the other half fell on the floor along with a lot of crumbs.

This day just kept getting better and better.

"Very funny, boys," she said. "But I'm afraid you'll have to sweep the floor now."

"Could we invent a sweeping machine to do the work quickly?" Orville asked.

"No," she said.

"Could we invite lots of people over and

attach scrubbers to the bottoms of their feet and turn on rock-and-roll music so that everybody would dance and scrub the floor at the same time?" I suggested.

"No!" she said.

"Could we train an army of cats to lick the floor clean?" Orville tried.

"NO!"

"Could we eat lunch first?" I asked.

"NO!!"

Orville begged, "Could you say something other than no?"

"Yes. Get busy."

"I like no better," Orville said. He went to the broom closet and pulled out the snow shovel.

We both cracked up.

Mom made macaroni and cheese and served it to us with toothbrushes from the fork drawer, of course. For dessert, I offered rocks from the candy box!

"No thank you," Mom said. "They look a little heavy. I'm on a diet."

"What are we going to do next, Wilbur?" Orville asked.

A great idea popped into my brain. "If we're switching *averything eround,* then today is a school day, and Mom has to go to school."

Orville grinned. "That means we get to be the principals."

You might not think that we, the *Biot Rrothers,* would want to go to school on a Saturday. But it's cool to go to school when no one else is there. Besides, Mom lets us play on the intercom.

Mom laughed. "I do have work I need to do in the school's computer lab. So we can go for an hour or two if you promise not to get in any trouble."

I looked at Orville. Orville looked at me.

"We never *tet* in any *grouble*," I said.

Orville gave his most angelic nod.

FOUR
Calling All Teachers

We bundled up and walked outside.

"Hey!" Margaret Lew called. She was playing with Jonathan Kemp in his yard. "Do you guys want to go sledding?"

Since we were switching things around, I decided we could tell everybody our mission. "It's *Dwitch Say*," I explained. "We're switching *averything eround*. So we're going to school today."

"We're going to be the principals," Orville added.

Our mom stepped out.

"Come along, Lydia," I said. "We're walking. And if you don't hurry, we'll be late!"

Jonathan and Margaret stared at us with their mouths open.

This happens to us a lot. People stare at us with their mouths open because we say and do such extraordinary things. If I were a germ, I'd follow me and Orville around all day because I'd have lots of opportunities to fly into people's mouths and land on their tonsils and give them sore throats.

I thought about this as we walked along. Maybe every time one of our friends gets sick, it's because we made their mouths drop open. I stopped. "Orville, we have a problem."

"What's that, Wilbur?"

"We make people's mouths drop open, and then germs fly in and make them sick. Don't look now, but it's happening to Margaret and Jonathan."

Orville did what any *Biot Rrother* would do. (Riot Brother Rule #3: If someone says, "Don't look now!" make sure you look.) Orville looked and gasped.

"What should we do?" I asked.

"I'll take care of it," Orville said. He turned around and shouted, "Germ alert! Close your mouths now!"

Margaret and Jonathan shut their mouths.

"Good work," I said.

Orville elbowed me and gestured to Mom. "Don't look now. But we have another problem."

Mom was staring at us with *her* mouth open!

I shook my head. "Close your mouth, Lydia. Didn't you hear anything we just said?"

Orville shook his head, too. "It's a good thing we're taking her to school. She has a lot to learn."

Mom laughed and said, "Did I really give birth to you guys?"

That's the funny thing about grown-ups. They often say things out of the blue.

When we got to school, Mom went to work in the computer lab. We sat in her office and did what any good principal would do. We put our feet up on the desk and made paper airplanes.

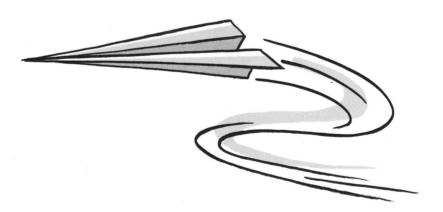

"What should we do after this, Principal Wilbur?" Orville asked as he flew an airplane across the room.

There was a knock on the window. On the snowy sidewalk outside stood Jonathan, Margaret, Alan, and Selena. They waved at us like they wanted to come in.

"Look, the teachers are here!" I said.

"Should we let them in?"

"*Nhy wot?*"

We opened the front door. "Since it's *Dwitch Say,* you're teachers," Orville said. "You can call us Principal Orville and Principal Wilbur."

"I always wanted to be a teacher!" Margaret said.

"Can I teach P.E., Principal Wilbur?" Alan asked.

"We're going to get in trouble, aren't we?" Selena asked.

"*Tet* in *grouble?*" Orville grinned. "How can you *tet* in *grouble* when we're the principals?"

Jonathan whispered, "Where'd you put your mom?"

"She's up on the second floor in the *lomputer cab*." I held open the door. "She won't even know you're here. Come into the office and take off your *cats* and *hoats*."

While the teachers were taking off their *cats* and *hoats*, I turned on the intercom. "Good morning, students. This is Principal Wilbur. Today is *Dwitch Say*. Please fall down and don't say the *Aledge* of *Pllegiance*. The teachers will be going to the gym to play! Over and out."

The teachers clapped.

I put a whistle around Alan's neck. "You're the P.E. teacher, Mr. Alan. What are we going to play today?"

Alan jumped up and down like a good P.E. teacher should. "Dodge Ball!"

"You mean *Bodge Dall*?"

Alan cackled, and everybody started walking to the gym.

"No walking in the halls!" Principal Orville said.

We ran.

As I was running, I was jingly on the inside and the outside. I was jingly on the inside because I was about to play an exciting game of *Bodge Dall.* I was jingly on the outside because I was holding Mom's keys.

Mom's keys open every room in the whole school—even the P.E. supply room. What's in the P.E. supply room, you ask? Most kids don't know. Jonathan, Alan, Margaret, and Selena didn't know. They waited breathlessly while I unlocked the door and turned on the light, and there it was . . . the cage!

FIVE

Haven't You Always Wanted to Be a Penguin?

I'm not kidding. There's a cage in the P.E. supply room. What's locked in the cage, you ask?

Children who have misbehaved? Wrong.

Pirates with missing limbs? Wrong.

Old rocket scientists with long beards? Wrong.

Trapeze artists who have fallen on their heads? Wrong.

I'm sorry to say that you are not a very good guesser.

Ha-ha—just kidding. I'm sure you are a *gabulous fuesser.* I'll tell you what's in the cage. One hundred and forty-four red rubber balls! They're like monkeys waiting to get out.

"I've never seen so many balls," Selena said.

"I think I'm going to faint with joy," Alan said.

"Principal Wilbur, how come our regular P.E. teacher only gives us a few at a time?" Margaret asked. "How come we don't get to play with all these at once?"

I shook my head sadly. "Most P.E. teachers don't know how to have fun." I grinned and unlocked the cage. "But Mr. Alan does! Right, Mr. Alan?"

"Let's play *Bodge Dall!*" Alan blew his whistle.

Six kids plus one hundred and forty-four balls is a real riot. *Bam! Bam! Boing! Boing!*

We *todged* and *dhrew* until we were exhausted.

"That was a fine P.E. class, Mr. Alan," Orville said. "Principal Wilbur and I are going to give you a raise."

"You are?"

"Of course," I said. We picked him up and threw him down on a mat.

Margaret jumped up. "I'm the art teacher, and we have art next. Let's go. We have *dork* to *wo*."

Using our artistic talents, we made a colorful new banner with block lettering and border illustrations to cover up the old banner about school rules. If you were in the art studio, you could have seen the real one. But since you weren't, I'll draw you a little one here.

NEW SCHOOL RULES

1. Teachers who crack funny jokes will get extra money.
2. Kids who crack funny jokes will get chocolate cupcakes.
3. Teachers who give homework will be sent to Alaska in their underpants.

While we were taping it up in the front hallway, Orville disappeared. A moment later, his voice came over the intercom. "Okay, teachers. *Lime* for *tunch*!"

"*Lime* for *tunch*!" I said. Even though we had already eaten lunch, it would be fun to go to the cafeteria.

"That is an *ixcellent edea*!" Margaret and the other teachers agreed.

Principal Orville joined us, and we ran to the cafeteria. We got lunch trays and stood in line.

"There's no food, Principal Wilbur," Selena said. "What'll we do?"

I looked out the window at the snow. A giant penguin of an idea was starting to burst out of my brain. Our school has a fabulous hill for sledding, and we were holding what might be the perfect sleds. I looked at my teachers. "If you don't have food, there's only one thing to do with a cafeteria tray.

Teachers, get your *cats* and *hoats*. We're *soing gledding*!"

Luckily, the windows of the computer lab don't face the hill, so we could sled on our cafeteria trays without that pesky Lydia Riot seeing us. We *flimbed* up the hill and *clew*

down. *Flimbed* up and *clew* down. Over and over until we were *wold* and *cet*.

"Time to dry off and relax," Orville said.

I nodded wisely. "There's only one place to go."

"Where?" Jonathan asked.

"The *leachers' tounge,* of course!"

SIX
Fun with *Sirty Docks!*

We ran to the teachers' lounge. I unlocked the door and opened it slowly. *"Leachers,* here is your *tounge,"* I said.

The teachers walked in and looked around.

"We've got couches!" Alan exclaimed.

"We've got a soda machine!" Margaret exclaimed.

"We've got a trash can!" Selena exclaimed.

"We have an appreciative staff," I exclaimed. "Don't we, Principal Orville?"

Orville grinned.

As we took off our boots, Jonathan whispered, "What do you think the real teachers do in here?"

"They pick their noses," Orville said.

"Then they smell their underarms," I said.

"Then they smoke cigars," Orville said.

"Then they take a nap." I stretched out on the couch and started snoring. "Guess who I am?"

"Mom!" Orville guessed.

"Right!"

Everybody laughed.

Orville sniffed my feet. "Whoa, Mom, your feet stink."

"Thank you," I said and wiggled my toes. "On *Dwitch Say*, it's good to have stinky feet."

My *sirty docks* were wet from playing in the snow. So I peeled them off, rolled them in a ball, and threw them in the air. To everybody's surprise, they landed in a trash can next to the vending machine.

"Two points!" Orville said.

Alan peeled off his socks and made a shot. I jumped up and blocked it, knocking his *sirty docks* across the room.

"*Sirty dockball*!" Orville yelled. Everybody took off his or her socks, rolled them into balls, and started playing our new version of basketball. Stinky sockballs were flying! Bare feet were jumping! Arms were flailing! Kids were shouting! It was a beautiful sight.

And then the door opened.

A flying sockball hit Mom right between the eyes.

Everybody froze.

"Lydia Riot," Orville said. "How many times have we told you to knock?"

Selena whispered, "I knew we'd get in trouble."

Luckily Mom was more surprised than mad. She told us that we should have asked her if it was okay to allow friends to play in the building.

"We're sorry," I said.

"We're *sery vorry*," Orville said.

"Next time we'll ask permission," I added.

Just then, an idea popped into my brain. "Speaking of asking for permission..." I whispered a question in my mom's ear.

Everyone waited breathlessly, wondering what brilliant plan was hatching in my great big head.

I finished whispering and let Mom think about it for a moment.

Everyone waited even more breathlessly, wondering if she'd say yes or no. Are you wondering? Well, hold your breath. If there's one thing I've learned in life, it's this: Don't rush grown-ups when they're deciding whether to give you permission to do something you really want to do. The brains of grown-ups work more slowly than kids' brains.

We were about to die of breathlessness when Lydia Riot finally spoke, "I must be crazy because the answer is yes!"

We whooped and hollered and jumped up and down.

"Wait a minute," Margaret said. "What was the question?"

"Are you ready?" I grinned and rubbed my hands together. "The question was, since it's *Dwitch Say,* can everybody sleep at our house instead of going to their own houses to sleep?"

"And the answer is yes!" Orville cried.

We whooped and hollered and jumped up and down until we ran out of breath again.

SEVEN
Let's *Bo* to the *Geach!*

Our mom called all our friends' parents and got permission. After all the moms and dads said yes, Orville couldn't stop jumping up and down. Thank goodness one of us remained calm.

"Okay," I said. "Everybody run home as fast as you can, get your *bleeping sags*, and meet us at our house."

"Don't forget toothbrushes," our mom said.

"That's exactly what my mom would say," Selena remarked.

Moms care about teeth. If they weren't already moms, they'd make great tooth fairies.

Orville and I ran home, too—even faster than our noses. We didn't have to pack our *bleeping sags* or toothbrushes, so we didn't have anything to do. We sat on the couch in the living room facing the door and waited. And waited. And waited.

"Wait!" I felt a saying coming on.

"I'm already waiting," Orville said politely.

I cleared my throat. "Time is an endless stream. To get across it, you have to do a lot of waiting. Waiting is like wading, get it?"

My brother nodded. "You're *wery vise*, Wilbur."

We waited some more. *Tick, tick, tick* went the clock.

"I think the clock is ticking more slowly than usual. Don't you agree, Orville?"

Orville nodded. "It always ticks more

slowly when we're waiting for friends to come over." He shook his fist at the clock. "Why are you so cruel to us, Mr. Clock? What did we ever do to you?"

Just then the clock chimed five times.

"Do you think it's trying to tell me something?" Orville asked.

"Yes. It's saying: It is five o'clock."

The door opened, and Orville jumped up.

Mom walked in. She was late because she hadn't run home like us.

"Oh crud, it's just you," Orville said.

"Thanks a lot," Mom said.

"We're waiting for our friends," I explained.

"I can see that," she said as she took off

her *hoat* and *cat*. "Why don't you do something to make the time pass more quickly? I think I'll go play my cello for a bit."

She left the room.

Orville sighed. "Wilbur, what can we do to make time pass more quickly?"

I thought for a moment. "Since it's *Dwitch Say* I think we need to do something to make time pass more *slowly*."

Orville groaned.

"Listen, Orville. It makes sense. If time passes more quickly, then it will be bedtime sooner. If time passes slowly, then we'll have more time to play with our friends."

Orville's big brown eyes lit up. *"Bongo bingo!"* he said. "But how do we make time pass more slowly?"

"Watch this." First I raised my eyebrows and flared my nostrils for dramatic effect. Then I slowly walked over to the big clock on our fireplace mantle and set the hands back one hour. "What time is it now, Orville?"

"Four o'clock, Wilbur."

"And what does that mean?"

"That means we will have an hour more to play with our friends!" he said. "You're right. That *does* make sense."

It was a good thing our mom was playing the cello because we were able to sneak around the house and set all the clocks back.

Finally, the doorbell rang and our friends arrived. Orville couldn't stop jumping up and down again, which made everybody else jump up and down. And then since it was

Dwitch Say, we decided to try jumping down and up instead of up and down. (See which way you think is the easiest.)

After a while, Mom stopped playing the cello and told us that if we kept jumping, we'd make the house fall down.

Making the house fall down sounded sort of exciting, but we actually like our house. So we decided to stop jumping and go outside and play *Gox* and *Feese*, which is what *Gox* and *Foose* is called when there is more than one *foose* on the loose. And that reminded us of another fun game to play in the snow called *Guck, Guck, Doose*. The *doose* is a close relative of the *foose*.

After playing those games we had dinner, which was really breakfast since it was *Dwitch Say*.

And what was for dinner, you ask? Cereal, toast, orange juice, and plenty of plastic bugs for playing Bye-Bye Buggie, of course.

After dinner, we had to decide what to do next.

"Since it's *Dwitch Say,* we should do

something that we don't ordinarily do in the winter," I suggested.

"Let's *bo* to the *geach*!" Orville said.

Everybody cheered.

"I don't think my mom will let me *bo* to the *geach* tonight," Jonathan said.

"So let's *bo* to the *gackyard*," I suggested. "Since we have snow instead of sand, we can build a snow castle."

Everybody cheered again.

One more time, we bundled up in our *cats* and *hoats* and went outside. It was dark, but the moon was bright. The snow was wet and

easy to pack. We gathered in a circle in the middle of the *gackyard*. We dug moats and shaped the snow into bridges, walls, staircases, turrets, and towers. Margaret found some broken fir tree branches, and we stuck these in the snow around the castle. They looked like real little trees.

After a while Mom came out. "Wow," she said.

We sat back and looked. It was a masterpiece, glistening in the moonlight.

"I have an idea!" Mom said. She went in and came out with two candles and some matches. She put one candle on top of the high tower. She put another one just inside the main entrance to the castle. She lit them and stepped back.

Golden light danced inside the castle, as if tiny people were having a party inside.

"It's perfect!" Jonathan said.

"It's the best thing I've ever seen," Margaret said.

"I can't believe we made it," Alan added.

"There's only one problem." Orville sighed. "My *fottom* is *brozen*!"

Everybody laughed.

A brilliant idea popped into my brain. "Since it's *Dwitch Say,* let's sit on beach chairs!"

Good old Mom helped us get the folding chairs out of the garage. We set them up in a circle around the castle.

A peaceful silence fell over us. It was a very still night: no wind in the treetops. One of our neighbors must have had a fire in his fireplace because we could smell the smoke—all toasty and warm—drifting through the cold, dark air.

Being at the beach at night is nice. But pretending that you are at the beach at night with your friends in your snowy *gackyard* is somehow even better.

Orville must have been thinking the same thing because he sighed and said, "This is the life."

I stretched out my arms and legs and tilted my face to the sky. "Hey everybody, let's see if we get a moontan!"

Everybody laughed.

Mom said, "You know you will have to go to bed at some point."

"We want to stay up until midnight," Orville said.

She shook her head. "Nope. Eleven o'clock at the latest."

"Come on, Mom. Be a pal," Orville said.

"Eleven o'clock," Mom said firmly.

Orville looked depressed. He forgot about switching the time on the clocks. I nudged him and whispered, "When the clock says eleven, it will really be midnight."

Orville leaned forward. "Mr. Clock is our friend."

"We definitely succeeded in our mission to switch things around today. Didn't we, Orville?"

"We're the *Biot Rrothers,*" Orville exclaimed with a grin. "Things always work according to our plan!" Triumphantly, he raised his arms and threw himself back in his chair. I don't think he planned the chair to tip, but it did. And he landed with a *thunk* in the snow.

Everybody laughed.

I, Wilbur Riot, being a very good brother, joined him.

The End

P.S. If you hang up a banner with new rules in your school, remember to take it down before Monday. Especially if the principal is your mother.

BONUS!

RIOT BROTHER GAMES

Bye—Bye Buggie

Say bye-bye to boredom by playing this delightful dinner table game! What are the rules, you ask? What supplies are needed? When is it best to play? If you'll stop asking so many questions, I'll tell you. First you need some bugs. (Hint, hint to any grown-ups reading this book: Fake bugs make excellent birthday presents.) During dinner, or lunch, or breakfast, try to flip a bug across the table without any grown-ups noticing. Use a spoon to catapult (or bugapult) the bug. Do not eat the bug. The goal is to make the lovely little creature land in someone else's food. You get 10,000 points every time this happens. When you're done, be neat and put your bugs away. (A good place is under your mom's pillow—ha ha.)

What's My Dumb Problem, Chum?

Get a partner. Pretend you have a big, dumb problem and act it out. For example, perhaps you're being sucked up by a vacuum cleaner, feet first. Or perhaps you've accidentally stuck your face in a beehive. You should use lots of sound effects, but you may not use any words or props. Your partner has to guess what your dumb problem is. Are you worried that you might not be able to think of anything to act out? Don't worry! If you're smart enough to read this book, then you're smart enough to think of lots of dumb problems! Take it from me.

Gox and Foose

We didn't invent this game, which is sometimes known as Fox and Goose or Fox and Geese, depending on how many people are playing. By the way, we do suggest that you play this game with human beings instead of geese. Real geese poop all over the place, which is annoying. This game is fun to play in the winter or at the beach. First you make a giant maze by scuffing your feet in a path through the snow or in the sand. Make sure the path has plenty of twists and turns and intersections and a few dead ends. The person who is the *gox* chases the person who is the *foose*. Players must always stay on the path. (If you're playing with human beings, you can be thankful that your path is not full of *poose goop*.) The *gox* has to make lots of sly faces and clawing gestures. The *foose* has to flap wings, honk loudly, and run for his or her life! As soon as the *gox* tags a *foose,* then the players switch roles. For a funny variation, try Reverse *Gox* and *Feese*: Everybody has to run backward! And the loser gets cooked (just kidding—*honk honk!*).

Guck, Guck, Doose

Winter Version: Sit in a circle in the snow. Each person makes one snowball and holds it in one hand. If you're "it," you tap the head of each player as you walk around the outside of the circle saying, *"Guck, Guck, Guck . . ."* When you get to the person you have chosen in your mind to be the *doose,* you squash your snowball on his or her head and yell, *"Doose!"* Then you run for your life around the circle. The *doose* has to try to hit you with his or her snowball before you sit back down. The good thing about this game is that it's really fun. The bad thing about this game is you freeze your bottom.

Summer Version: You can play this on the beach, too. Instead of snowballs you need cups of water. If you're "it," you tap all the *gucks.* When you get to the *doose,* pour your cup of water on the person's head. The *doose* has to try to splash you with the water in his or her cup before you sit down. The good thing about this game is that getting splashed with water really cools you off. The bad thing about this game is ... hey, there isn't anything bad about this game!

Sirty Dockball

Have you ever wondered what to do when your laundry basket is overflowing with stinky, dirty socks? Play *Sirty Dockball*. Roll up your socks into tight balls. Try to shoot your sockballs into a trash can while blocking your opponent. Whoever has the stinkiest socks wins. Just kidding—ha ha! Whoever gets the most baskets wins. The loser has to wear the other person's stinky socks to school (*not* kidding—ha ha!).

ADDITIONAL RIOT BROTHER RULES

11. Do not tell grown-ups how to play secret games.
12. If one person is about to get in trouble, the other person must create a distraction outside the nearest window.

13. Whoever wakes up first has to wake the other.
14. You have to dance and squawk like a plucked chicken every time you break a rule.
15. You can't do the same mission twice.

RIOT BROTHER SAYINGS

—Riots are the best medicine.

—A riot a day keeps boredom away.

—Don't have a cow—have a riot! (Unless you need the milk.)

—There's nothing like going to breakfast with bugs hidden in your pocket to get the day off to a great start.

—Life is boring when you're not spying on someone.

—A bad day is like bad breath. It just gets worse unless you do something about it.

—You should always laugh before you go to bed. If you have to go to bed before you've had a good laugh, try to crack yourself up first!

—Sleeping at night is bad enough. But sleeping in the morning is just plain ridiculous.

—Snot and kids have a lot in common. When the weather is cold and snowy, they both like to come out and play.

—Time is an endless stream. To get across it, you have to do a lot of waiting.